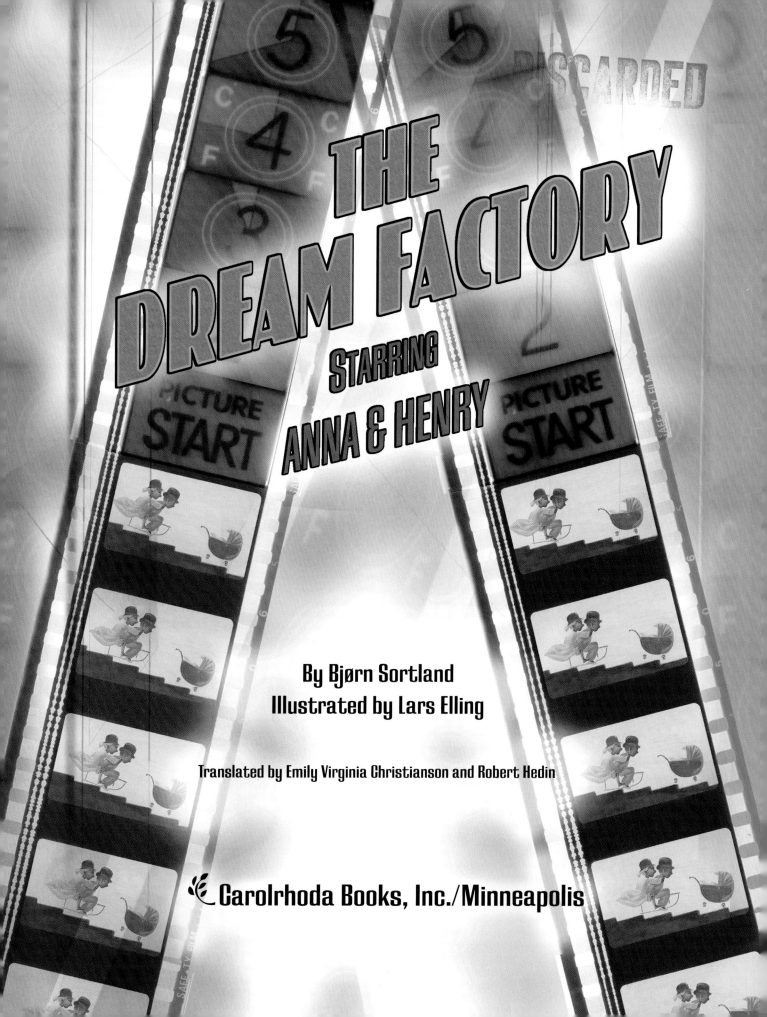

THE DREAM FACTORY

STARRING ANNA & HENRY

By Bjørn Sortland
Illustrated by Lars Elling

Translated by Emily Virginia Christianson and Robert Hedin

Carolrhoda Books, Inc./Minneapolis

Anna sighed. "Christmas Eve is over in a second. All the packages are opened," she said to her brother, Henry.

"If it's an important second, a second can last a long time," Uncle Paul reminded them. "Anyway, there's one present you haven't opened yet. It's up in the attic. I have wrapped it in a riddle:

> *Legs as sharp as blades.*
> *Sometimes for grown-ups,*
> *But mostly for children.*
> *What am I?*

Anna and Henry racked their brains.

"A pony!" exclaimed Anna, who wanted a horse for Christmas.

Henry grinned at her. "A pony? Nooo, it sounds more like . . . well, like stilts?"

"You'll just have to go up to the attic to see for yourselves, my little rosebuds," said Uncle Paul. "But, remember, it's better to give than to receive—especially at Christmas. Here, take this candle. It's awfully dark up there."

Henry took the candle and headed up the big, creaky stairs to the attic. Anna followed behind, trembling a little as Henry slowly opened the door. The attic was creepy and cold, and the candle cast long, eerie shadows on the walls and ceiling. What kind of present could possibly be up here?

"Uncle Paul is the oddest of all our uncles," said Henry. "Only he would think of wrapping a present in a riddle. And why did he call us little rosebuds?"

"Look here!"

said Anna. "Two cool hats! Let's try them on."

Anna and Henry put on the hats, and suddenly the candle went out. The attic was pitch black and very quiet. Something incredible

and exciting

and dreadful

was about to happen.

But what?

"It's as dark in here as the inside of a bag,"
Henry said without uttering a sound. Instead
his words appear inside this frame.

"Yes. So dark that I can't hear a word,"
Anna said to herself.

Henry grabbed a
corner of the darkness. It
felt like canvas and was
as big as a movie screen.
He tugged it back!

"Where in the world are we?" Anna wondered aloud. She had her voice back and was glad to see light again.

"Welcome!" said a little man with a hat, mustache, and cane. "How wonderful that you're already wearing your pajamas. We always have dreams waiting for you here at the Dream Factory."

"And such stylish hats you're wearing! I'm all out of canes but, here, take these umbrellas instead."

"Legs as sharp as blades . . ." Anna began. "Could Uncle Paul's Christmas present be umbrellas?"

"I don't know,"
the man said, shrugging his shoulders.
"I'm only the director here."

"You mean, you work here at the
Dream Factory?" asked Henry.

"Yes, that's right. What kind of
dreams would you like?"

"Something with horses," Anna
quickly replied. "Maybe a pon—"

Before she
could say
anything more,
the man yelled,

"Cut! CUT! Horse scene!

Here you go!" And
then he was gone.

All at once everything
changed, and Anna and Henry
found themselves standing in a
chariot pulled by a team of
strong horses.

"Things certainly go faster here than they do in the real world," Anna giggled to herself. She struggled to keep her balance in the chariot.

"We're in one of those old silent movies," hollered Henry, who looked like a blur.

The crowd surrounding them looked as if they were shouting and roaring, but all Anna or Henry could hear was total silence. Then, before they knew what was happening, they heard a loud Tarzan yell, and someone lifted them high into the air!

AAAAAAAAAIAIAIAIAIAAAAA!

Henry hoped that Tarzan was really as strong as he was supposed to be. Anna felt butterflies in her stomach as she clung desperately to the tip of the umbrella.

"CUT!" Anna yelled.

But it didn't help. And they almost fell straight into the jaws of a crocodile.

"Help," whispered Henry.

"What's going on here?" Now they were staring deep into the black eyes of what must have been the world's largest ape!

"I hope this is just a movie trick," said Anna.

The ape picked her up and sniffed her a little.

"Cut! CUT!" Anna shouted again. But again nothing helped.

"Listen, I am the King of the Apes. Really I am," said Tarzan meekly. "So you'd better let us go."

And that was exactly what the big ape did! He let them go . . . and down they tumbled through the air!

"Open your umbrella!" Henry called to Anna, as they

fell and fell and fell and fell...

. . . until they landed softly in a street. Whatever happened to Tarzan, they didn't know.

"Maybe taking these umbrellas wasn't such a bad idea," said Henry, rubbing his eyes. "Is this really real, or just a crazy dream?"

"At last, some color and music," said Anna, her heart beating a little slower now. They paused to watch a man dance and sing in the pouring rain.

"I'm singin' in the rain, just singin' in the rain," the man sang happily. He was soaking wet.

Henry shook his head. "Let's not bother him. He wouldn't know anyway. We still haven't found what we're looking for."

"Henry, we don't even know what we're looking for," said Anna. "Besides, we're getting soaked ourselves."

"RIDDLES AND TEA," read Henry on a sign over a door. "Let's go in here."

"Cool! Everything here is just like a cartoon," exclaimed Anna. "Nothing too scary could happen to us here."

"It is not polite to come as an uninvited guest to an **un-birthday** party." The March Hare looked at them. "Would you like some tea?"

"Yes, thank you," Henry replied, "but only half a cup, please. Say, whose birthday is it?"

"No one's. We're all celebrating **un-birthdays,**" explained a little mouse, popping his head out of the teapot. "There are 365 days in a year. Only one of those is your birthday. Therefore, the other 364 days are un-birthdays," he said.

"Tell me, how are a raven and a desk alike?" asked the man with the hat.

"A riddle!" said Henry. "Let's see, hmmm. . . . Could it be—"

"No, no, no," said the March Hare. "Are you stark raving mad? We never tell the answers to riddles here."

"Yes, you must tell us," Anna said firmly. "We have a riddle ourselves."

"I'm late, I'm late," said the March Hare and bounded away.

"Let's go, Anna," said Henry.

"Only tea and nonsense here," Anna sighed, and she pulled back a curtain hanging nearby.

"Look! There's a tea party in this room, too," whispered Anna. "But the guests all look sad."

Henry cleared his throat.

"Excuse us for disturbing your tea party, but we're wondering if you could solve a riddle for us?"

No one said a word. Henry cleared his throat again.

"Legs as sharp as blades. Sometimes for grown-ups, but mostly for children. What am I?" he asked cautiously.

No one answered. Then one of them got out a sheet of paper and a pen, and they all began to whisper among themselves. "Do you think they understand the riddle?" asked Anna.

But before she could finish her question, the man took the pen and guided it smoothly and elegantly across the paper, then showed them the character he had drawn.

"I don't really know what this means," said Anna as she studied the drawing. "I've just started school, and we haven't gotten to Japanese yet."

"We should thank them anyway," Henry said as he bowed and dragged Anna through the first door he saw.

"Shhh!

We mustn't wake them," said Henry.

Anna and Henry had found themselves standing in a dark room. Close by, dressed in pajamas, a girl and a boy lay in bed.

"Can't wake me!" exclaimed the boy, jumping up. "I'm not sleeping. Are you, Fanny?"

"No," said the girl. "Get out of bed, Alexander, and show them the wonderful gift you got for Christmas!"

"A magic lantern," announced the boy. He lit a candle inside a small lamp, and suddenly something almost magical began to happen. Large pictures appeared on the wall, some moving slowly. In a hushed voice, the boy began to tell a scary story.

"You should become a storyteller when you grow up," said Anna, who thought the story was very creepy.

Just then the door opened. Anna and Henry burrowed under the covers.

"For the third time, go to sleep!" a woman's voice warned. Then, thankfully, the door closed again.

"We got a Christmas present, too," said Henry. "But we have no idea what it is."

Henry repeated the riddle.

"That's easy," the girl replied. "It's—"

The boy stopped her. "Let them find out for themselves," he said and blew out the candle.

"Go through that door. There, at least, you'll find some snow."

As they came through the door, they found wind and driving snow, but things still didn't seem right. The snow was cotton and tasted terrible. The wind was warm.

They sought shelter in a cabin, where they discovered that someone was already there. He was eating an old shoe. It was the same man they'd met behind the dark canvas!

"Doesn't that taste awful?" asked Anna.

"Not really," the man said, smiling. "Actually, this shoe is made of licorice. The problem is that the director is never satisfied, so I have to eat the same shoe over and over again. I'm going crazy!"

"But aren't you the director?"

"Well, yes," the man replied.

"We're beginning to go crazy ourselves searching for the answer to our riddle," said Anna. "We don't want to be here in the Dream Factory anymore."

The man gave Henry a sly look. "Chicken," the man said.

"What do you mean? The answer to our riddle is chicken?"

"Chicken, chicken," replied the man, waving his knife and fork in Henry's direction.

"He's only kidding," said Anna.

"Let's go," said Henry, who was not so sure and was eager to get home. He grabbed a sled leaning against the wall.

Anna and Henry leapt out into the cottonlike snow. They were about to throw themselves onto the sled, but they were stopped by a flight of stairs. Just as they began to descend the slippery steps, Anna paused.

"Wait a second!" she said. "Something is written on this sled."

"Hurry up!" said Henry. "I want to get home!"

"**Rosebud,**" read Anna.

"What?"

Now Henry stopped, too.

"Uncle Paul is so clever!" Anna said. "It's right here: Legs as sharp as blades. Sometimes for grown-ups, but mostly for children. . . . A sled. How simple! The answer to the riddle is a sled. A sled called Rosebud!"

Henry looked at Anna. "I didn't know you were so smart," he said.

"A fine present," said Anna.

"But hard to come by," mumbled Henry. "Uncle Paul is certainly odd, but that man with the mustache is completely crazy! Let's get out of here. No way do I want to be a chicken dinner!"

"Shhh, don't make a sound," whispered Anna.

Before they had gone very far, they heard some scary music in the distance. And as it grew louder, it grew scarier and scarier.

Henry looked back over his shoulder. He felt that something strange was about to happen.

And it did. They heard something coming. Something clattering.

"Look! An old baby carriage!" yelled Henry.

"We have to save that baby!" screamed Anna.

Quick as lightning, they jumped onto Rosebud. They whizzed and bumped down the stairs so fast that sparks flew off the runners.

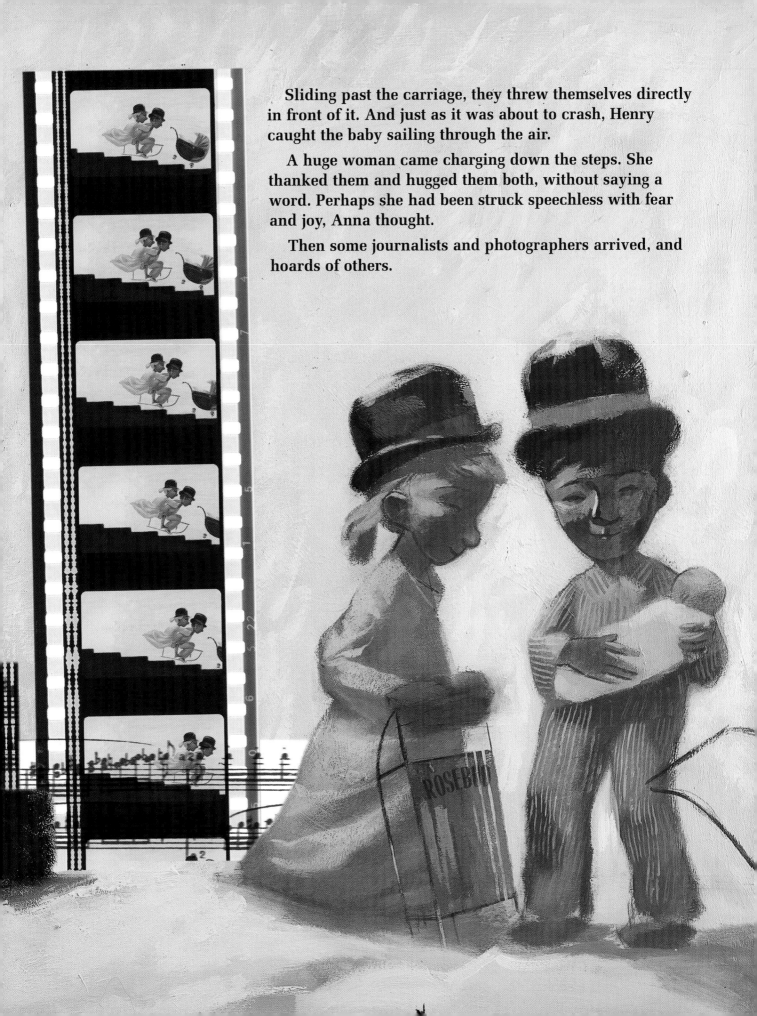

Sliding past the carriage, they threw themselves directly in front of it. And just as it was about to crash, Henry caught the baby sailing through the air.

A huge woman came charging down the steps. She thanked them and hugged them both, without saying a word. Perhaps she had been struck speechless with fear and joy, Anna thought.

Then some journalists and photographers arrived, and hoards of others.

AT THE L

ODESSA(AP):
Yesterday evening during
filming, two fast-thinking
children saved a newborn
baby as its carriage rolled out
of control down the stairs. In

c
end

When a
young her
movies that
endings."

OO XOXO OO
XOXO OO OX
OO XOXO OOOOOX XX OO XOXOOOX
XOXOX XX OO XOXO XOXOOOX OO XOXOX
XOXO OKOXOXOX OO XOXO XOXOOOXOXOX OO XX
XOXO OKOXOOOX OO XOXO OOOX OO XOXO OOOX
XX OO XOXOOOX OO XOXO XOXOOOX OO XX
OO XOXO OO XOXOOOX OO
OO XOXO OO XOXO

OO XOXO OO OX
XX OO XOX

NEW YORK

Inquirer

Mandag 20. september 1941

...AST SECOND!!

...just a split second, when the
two heroes jumped onto a sled
...and rescued the child, they
...ated a new and surprising
...g to an old and sad story.
...ed to comment, the
...s said, "We like
...ve happy

"My Rosebud," uttered an old man who sat alone in his castle. Around him were hundreds of thousands of crates and cartons, stuffed crocodiles, statues of horses, suits of armor, and almost everything else you could find in the world.

"My Rosebud . . ."

The old man studied the photo of the sled in the newspaper long and hard.

"I must meet these two young heroes," he said to himself.

"How did we end up here?" asked Henry. He and Anna were standing before the old man.

"A little movie magic. I once was very good at it," the old man said.

"Why did you bring us here?"

"You two have something that I want more than anything else in the world," sighed the old man. "You have my Rosebud."

"The sled?" said Henry. "But it's *our* present. And, to be quite honest, we had to work awfully hard to find it." The man looked at them, his eyes dark and sad.

"Why do you want this sled more than anything else in the world?" Anna asked him.

"Many people have wondered about that. It seems I have everything, everything in the whole world. But the only time I was really happy was when I was a child. And then I had only one thing—**my Rosebud.**"

"Merry Christmas!" exclaimed Anna. And before Henry could stop her, she handed him the sled.

"Thank you, my children," he said. "Here. I want you to have this gift in return."

It was a small clear ball. An old-fashioned snow globe!

"Cut," said the old man. All at once the lights went out, and a gust of wind blew off their hats.

Once again, Anna and Henry were surrounded by pitch black. And quiet.

Henry groped in the dark until he discovered a doorknob. Carefully, he opened the door . . . and heard his mother, father, Uncle Harold, Uncle Richard, and Uncle Paul down in the living room, talking and laughing. He and Anna were back in the attic. They went through the door

and

down

the

stairs.

"Strange as it seems," Henry said to Anna, "that old man was as happy as a boy when you gave him the sled. I wonder if Uncle Paul will be mad when we tell him that you gave away our present?"

"Remember, Henry, it's better to give than to receive, and especially at Christmas," Anna said. "Besides, I don't like stories with sad endings."

Anna and Henry looked at each other and smiled.

"Just think, tomorrow when I wake up I'll be in my own bed," yawned Henry. "Tonight I don't want to dream of anything at all. Do you think it was just a dream, Anna?"

Anna paused. "Look in the snow globe, Henry. Who do you think those children inside *really* are?"

The End

Here are the actors and films that Anna and Henry encountered on their adventure:

Charlie Chaplin (1889–1977),

the man with the hat, mustache, and cane, is one of the most famous names in the world of film. Englishman Charles Spencer Chaplin did it all. He was an actor, producer, director, composer, and screenwriter. He grew up in the theater and was a professional dancer on the London stage by the time he was nine years old. Later, he traveled to the United States and had great success appearing as "The Tramp" in many films. The Tramp—a simple, naive character who always wins out against great odds while displaying elegant humor—is one of the best-known and best-loved characters in film history. The picture on the cover of this book is from *The Kid* (1921), one of Chaplin's most famous films. Anna and Henry meet Charlie again during the filming of *The Gold Rush* (1925), Chaplin's masterpiece.

Al Jolson (1886–1950)

was one of the movies' greatest singing stars. He played the title role in *The Jazz Singer* (1927), the first successful film made with sound. With the opening line of the film: "Wait a minute, wait a minute, you ain't heard nothin' yet," the history of films was changed forever. It left audiences demanding more, and sound pictures had come to stay. In this book, Al Jolson appears on the poster in Uncle Paul's attic.

Friedrich Murnau (1888–1931)

was the director of *Nosferatu* (1922), one of the first horror movies ever made. Max Schreck (1879–1936) played the title role in this silent film about a vampire named Count Orlak *(left)* who terrorizes a small German village. Friedrich Murnau created many film techniques that later influenced the work of other directors.

Laurel and Hardy

are the two men in this book who wear derby hats and carry scenery for the background. Plump Oliver Hardy (1892–1957) and skinny Stan Laurel (1890–1965) were one of the most successful comedy teams to ever appear on film, and they performed together in more than a hundred movies.

Marlene Dietrich (1901–1992)

was a beautiful, mysterious German actress who was famous all over the world. She is best known for the film *Blue Angel* (1930). She was also a successful cabaret singer and recording artist. Because she refused to work for the Nazis in World War II, her films were banned in Germany. This only served to increase her popularity throughout the world.

Ben-Hur

is a film about a man named Ben-Hur, a Jew who fights to save his people from the tyranny of the Romans. He is a contemporary of Jesus, and there are many similarities between the two. But when Ben-Hur finally meets Jesus, he changes to find a more peaceful way to fight the Romans. *Ben-Hur—Stories of Jesus* (1926), directed by Fred Niblo (1874–1948), is a silent film with elaborate life-size sets and thousands of actors and technicians. By far the most famous scene of the film is the chariot race. In this book, Anna and Henry can be seen in the chariot of Ben-Hur, here played by Ramon Novarro (1899–1968). Charlton Heston (1924–) starred in the award-winning remake of the film in 1959.

Johnny Weismuller (1904–1984)

was one of many actors who played the role of Tarzan the Ape Man on film. But Weismuller, a five-time Olympic swimming gold medalist, was by far the most famous. People often still imitate Weismuller's Tarzan call—a loud yell mixed with a yodel. In our book, he takes Anna and Henry on a short tour of the jungle.

King Kong (1933)

is a film about a giant ape that is discovered on a remote island. He is then taken to civilization and put on public display. He falls in love with a human woman and manages to escape. King Kong may be a monster, but he still has feelings! At the end of the movie, he dies at the top of the Empire State Building in New York City. *King Kong* was a huge success, with special effects far ahead of their time.

Metropolis (1926)

is a science fiction film by German director Fritz Lang (1890–1976). The movie is famous for its futuristic set designs and special effects, its interplay of light and shadow, and its rhythmic pace. *Metropolis* is also an example of how artistic movements—in this case the expressionist style—can be represented in film, art, and literature.

D. W. Griffith (1875–1948),

one of the most influential directors and producers in American movie history, helped make film an important art form. He is estimated to have made between 400 and 500 films, most of them very short movies. Griffith is best known for his two epic films, *Birth of a Nation* (1915) and *Intolerance* (1916).

Gene Kelly (1912–1996)

co-directed and played the lead role in one of the best-loved movie musicals ever made, *Singin' in the Rain* (1951). The story takes place in Hollywood at the time when silent film stars were forced to make the transition to "talkies," movies with sound. One of the most-famous scenes in all of film history is the scene in which Gene Kelly falls happily in love and ends up singing and dancing in the rain.

Alice in Wonderland (1951)

is an animated film by the Walt Disney film studios, based on a world-famous book by English writer Lewis Carroll (1832–1898). Just like Anna and Henry, Alice discovers that she can go from the real world to a fantasy world, a realm where many incredible and exciting things happen.

The Seven Samurai

was a film made in 1954 by the internationally known Japanese director Akira Kurosawa (1910–1998). The film deals with how the seven title characters, professional warriors, save a small village from bandits. *The Seven Samurai* is a classic that has inspired countless filmmakers. In 1960 it was remade as an American Western called *The Magnificent Seven.*

Ingmar Bergman (1918–)

is a Swedish director who worked in both films and theater. Bergman often addressed moral and religious themes in his films, and many of his movies were influenced by his childhood and his upbringing as a minister's son. In this book, Anna and Henry encounter Fanny and Alexander, the main characters in a 1983 movie of the same name.

Potemkin

is a silent film made in 1925 by the famous Russian director Sergei M. Eisenstein (1898–1948). Eisenstein developed an important method of editing film known as the montage technique, in which scenes are arranged to suggest a symbolic meaning. The most famous scene of the film occurs on the Odessa Steps, in Ukraine, and it is here that Anna and Henry jump in and change history. As a film is projected, 24 pictures are shown every second—the number needed to create the illusion of natural movement.

Orson Welles (1915–1985)

was a versatile American actor and director, and the film *Citizen Kane* (1941) is considered his masterpiece. Welles played the title role, of a publisher who rises to great power. *Citizen Kane* is an important contribution to film history, largely because Welles, in making the film, created camera techniques that went on to influence the work of many other directors. *Citizen Kane* is the story of one of the world's richest men, a person who has everything but what he wants most: the simple joy he experienced as a boy with his sled, Rosebud.

Anna and Henry

are a sister and brother who find themselves taking part in films that were made long before they were even born. But, right now, they definitely need to go to bed. Good night!

About the Author and Illustrator

Bjørn Sortland is the author of two other books featuring Anna and Henry: *Anna's Art Adventure* (called "a merry tale" in a *Kirkus* pointer review) and *The Story for the Search for the Story,* a journey through the world of literature. Sortland's highly acclaimed works of fiction have been translated into many languages.

Lars Elling earned several awards for his first book, *Anna's Art Adventure,* including Norway's Gold Medal for Illustration. He has since illustrated a number of books, published in his native Norway and around the world, including *The Story of the Search for the Story* by Bjørn Sortland, and *The Faithful Bull* by Ernest Hemingway.

About the Translators

Emily Virginia Christianson is a native of Red Wing, Minnesota, and a graduate of Carleton College in Northfield, Minnesota. She first learned Norwegian as a child, studying at the Concordia Language Villages, St. Olaf College, and Seljord Folkehogskule in the Telemark district of Norway. She currently teaches Norwegian to children.

Robert Hedin is the author, translator, and editor of twelve books of poetry and prose, most recently *The Old Liberators: New and Selected Poems and Translations.* He has taught at colleges and universities across the country and currently directs the Anderson Center for Interdisciplinary Studies in Red Wing, Minnesota.

Carolrhoda Books, Inc.
A division of Lerner Publishing Group
241 First Avenue North, Minneapolis, MN 55401 U.S.A.

Website address: www.lernerbooks.com

Library of Congress Cataloging-in-Publication Data

Sortland, Bjørn
[24 i sekundet. English]
    The dream factory starring Anna & Henry / by Bjørn Sortland ;
illustrated by Lars Elling ; translated by Emily Virginia Christianson
and Robert Hedin.
        p.   cm.
    Summary: While searching for a special Christmas present, Anna and
Henry are pulled into a magical movie world, meet famous film
personalities, and have a chance to change movie history.
    ISBN: 0–87614–009–6 (lib. bdg. : alk. paper)
    [1. Motion pictures—Fiction. 2. Christmas—Fiction.] I. Elling,
Lars, ill. II. Christianson, Emily Virginia. II. Hedin, Robert, 1949– .
IV. Title.
PZ7.S7218 Dr 2001
[E]—dc21   00–012659

Manufactured in the United States of America
1 2 3 4 5 6 – JR – 06 05 04 03 02 01